ISBN: 9798861710374

This book is dedicated to our little friends from the "Friendship Club." Your incredible journeys, boundless curiosity, and unwavering compassion have inspired every page. As we ventured alongside Bouncy Bear and Curious Cat, we learned invaluable lessons from the kiddos we worked with.

Your unique perspectives have been our greatest teachers, showing us the beauty of understanding, empathy, and embracing differences. May this book serve as a small tribute, filled with the hope that it will inspire kindness, compassion and social skills tools in the hearts of all who read it.

With heartfelt gratitude and admiration,

Yrenka Lolli-Sunderlin and Gavin Sunderlin

Bouncy Bear is a lively and friendly resident of the enchanting forest. He is always full of energy and loves to go on exciting adventures with his best friend, Curious Cat. Bouncy Bear's enthusiasm and kindness makes him a beloved member of the forest community, and he is always ready to lend a helping paw to his friends. Together with Curious Cat, Bouncy Bear explores the forest and learns important social skills lessons.

Curious Cat is a friendly forest dweller who lives in the enchanting forest. Always filled with questions and wonder, Curious Cat is known for his inquisitive nature. He is best friends with Bouncy Bear and together, they embark on exciting adventures to make new friends. Curious Cat's curiosity leads them to discover new flexible ways to think. With his warm heart and a desire to learn, Curious Cat is a cherished member of the forest community.

Once upon a bright morning in the colorful forest, Bouncy Bear and Curious Cat were playing their favorite game, "Imagination Tag." They loved pretending to be characters from fairy tales, and they laughed joyfully as they ran through the woods.

As they played, they came upon their friend, Thoughtful Turtle, sitting under a big oak tree, looking upset.

"Hi, Thoughtful Turtle! What's bothering you?" asked Curious Cat with concern.

Thoughtful Turtle sighed. "I keep getting sticky thoughts whenever something doesn't go the way I thought it would be. It's hard to let go, and it makes me feel really sad and anxious."

Bouncy Bear nodded. "We understand, Thoughtful Turtle. But don't worry! We can help you train your brain to be more flexible like a rubber band."

Curious Cat added, "Just like when we play 'Imagination Tag,' we can use our visualization skills to come up with new ways to handle sticky thoughts."

They sat with Thoughtful Turtle and shared their own experiences of dealing with sticky thoughts. Bouncy Bear talked about the time when he couldn't bounce as high as he wanted and felt disappointed. Curious Cat shared how he felt frustrated when his blocks fell down before he finished building a tower.

"But," said Curious Cat, "we found different ways to have fun and feel better. We can teach you how!"

Bouncy Bear chimed in, "Yes! Flexible thinking is like having a superpower that helps us bounce back from sticky thoughts!"

Together, they embarked on a flexible thinking journey.
Whenever one of them had a sticky thought, they would all
take turns coming up with new ideas.

When Thoughtful Turtle thought he couldn't draw as well as bouncy bear, Curious Cat suggested, "What if you try using different colors and shapes? Your drawing will be uniquely beautiful!" Bouncy Bear added, "And if you need help, we'll be here to support you, just like you support us when we play games together."

He discovered that he could replace sticky thoughts with more positive and creative ones.

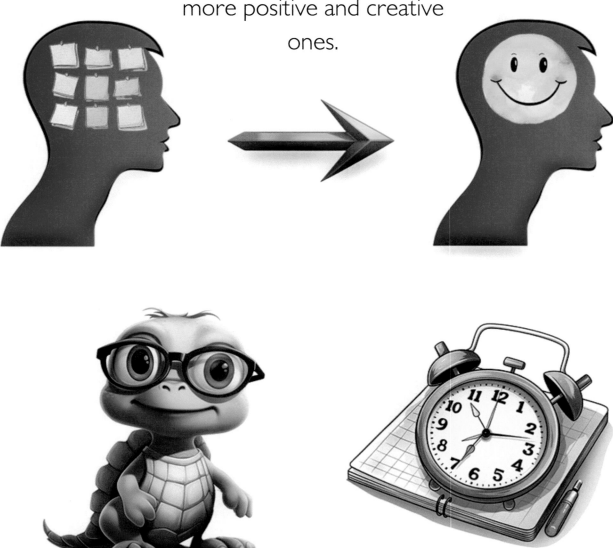

As the days went by, Thoughtful Turtle's mind felt lighter and freer. He realized accepting things as they are and letting go of "sticky thoughts" help him make and keep friends.

One day, they encountered a big fallen log blocking their path to the sparkling stream. Thoughtful Turtle began to worry, "How will we cross it? We'll never get to the stream now. But Curious Cat smiled. "Let's put our flexible thinking caps on! We can find a way together."

Bouncy Bear suggested, "Maybe we can go around the log and take a different path." Curious Cat added, "Or we could work as a team and lift the log together!" Thoughtful Turtle hesitated but then remembered his friends' advice. "I have a new idea! What if we use the log as a bridge and cross over it?"

And so, with a bit of teamwork and a lot of flexible thinking, they crossed the log and reached the sparkling stream, celebrating their success with high fives and laughter.

Their flexible thinking journey continued, and soon the whole forest noticed the positive change in Thoughtful Turtle. Animals would seek his advice when they had sticky thoughts of their own. Thoughtful Turtle felt happy to make new friends.

As the seasons passed, the friends remained steadfast, supporting one another through every challenge. Their forest family grew, and they learned that by embracing flexibility, they could turn sticky thoughts into stepping stones toward happiness and success.

Dear young friend!

Let's practice flexible thinking together! When sticky thoughts pop up, use your imagination to find new ways to solve problems. Draw a picture of a sticky thought you've had recently. Now, beside it, draw three creative and flexible solutions. Remember, there's no wrong answer!

Example: Sticky Thought: "I don't know what to say to make new friends." Flexible Solutions:

1. Ask questions: When you meet someone new, ask them about their favorite hobbies or interests. This can start a fun conversation!

2. Share your interests: Talk about the things you love. You might find someone who likes the same things.

3. Join a group: Participate in clubs or activities that interest you. You'll meet friends who already share your passions!

With flexible thinking, you can turn sticky thoughts into positive ways to make new friends. Just like Bouncy Bear, Curious Cat, and Thoughtful Turtle, you can overcome any social challenge!

I am a Flexible Thinker:

1) I am having a sticky thought!

My sticky thought is: _____

2) If I am upset, I can use my words to express my feelings!

I feel: _____ when:_____

3) I can use my coping skills to help me calm down!

I can: _____

4) I can be a flexible thinker by trying something new!

I can: _____

I feel happier when
I put on my flexible thinking cap, because it helps me have fun with
my friends!

My Flexible Thinking Journal

_____

_____

_____

_____

_____

_____

_____

Yrenka Lolli-Sunderlin is an experienced behavior analyst with 29 years of expertise in providing social skills groups for children, teen and young adults. Originally from Pasadena, California, she currently resides in Meridian, Idaho. Yrenka is deeply passionate about two subjects: teaching coping skills and social skills. This passion led her to embark on her first project, where she collaborated with her son, Gavin Sunderlin.

In addition to this project. Yrenka is avidly interested in AI prompting engineering, continuously seeking ways to enhance her field of expertise. She is particularly proud of her achievements in her private practice as a behavior analyst, where she has made a lasting impact on the lives of many individuals.

About the Content Creator

Find more of her work:
@the_yrenka_method

Gavin Sunderlin is from Meridian, Idaho, and has roots in Pasadena, California. His diverse background and experiences have greatly influenced the themes and content of the art direction of this book. Gavin draws inspiration from his career as a behavior therapist, working with children with special needs. This background has driven his passion for creating meaningful and impactful visual content.
In addition to his work, Gavin has a keen interest in automotive journalism and AI engineering. His multifaceted interests reflect his curiosity and the depth of his expertise

Find more of his work:
@gavins_ai_creations

About the Art Director

Co-Creator

Made in United States
Troutdale, OR
02/16/2024

17711883R00017